Quacky Baseball

Peter
Abrahams

Illustrated by
Frank Morrison

HARPER
An Imprint of HarperCollinsPublishers

Quacky Baseball
Text copyright © 2011 by Pas de Deux
Illustrations copyright © 2011 by Frank Morrison
All rights reserved. Manufactured in China.
No part of this book may be used or reproduced in any manner whatsoever without written permission except
in the case of brief quotations embodied in critical articles and reviews. For information address HarperCollins
Children's Books, a division of HarperCollins Publishers, 10 East 53rd Street, New York, NY 10022.
www.harpercollinschildrens.com

Library of Congress Cataloging-in-Publication Data is available.
ISBN 978-0-06-122978-7 (trade bdg.) — ISBN 978-0-06-122979-4 (lib. bdg.)

Typography by Jennifer Rozbruch
11 12 13 14 15 SCP 10 9 8 7 6 5 4 3 2 1
❖
First Edition

To my sons, Seth and Ben,
who taught me the game

—P.A.

To my heavy hitters,
Nyree, Tyreek, Nia, and Nasir

—F.M.

Opening day—

and Thumby Duckling is nervous.

Thumby is making his very first start for the Webbies.

INNING	1	2	3	4	5	6	7	8	9	RUNS
QUACKERS	0	0	1	0	0	0	0	0	2	3
WEBBIES	0	0	0	0	0	0	0	0		0

Been a long day at the ball field.

Top of the ninth. Two on,
two out for the Quackers.
The Webbies need an out!

Thumby makes the catch! Out number three.

How about that!

Bottom of the ninth—last chance for the Webbies.
Leading off, Speedy O'Duck.
Speedy bunts, and...

it's a beauty. Safe at first!

INNING	1	2	3	4	5	6	7	8	9	RUNS
QUACKERS	0	0	1	0	0	0	0	2	0	3
WEBBIES	0	0	0	0	0	0	0	0		0

On deck—Canardo Duck,
who goes down swinging.

Bunting Tip: Bunt down on the ball!

Stepping up to the plate,

Flakey Duckstein.

Flakey's new to the team. Just flew in yesterday.

Flakey singles up the middle!

And Speedy scoots
all the way to third.

Ducks on first and third. The Webbies aren't out of this yet.

Now batting, Medwick Ducky. He can tie the game with one swing of that mighty bat.

Baserunning Tip: Don't look back!

But no.

Steeee-rike three!

Two on, two out for Manny El Pato. The crowd is going wild.

Here comes the pitch.

Uh-oh...duck!

Manny heads down to first, hit by the pitch.
And that loads the bases with two out.
Last chance for the Webbies.

And the next batter is...

Thumby Duckling!

What a moment for the little rookie from the wrong side of the marsh.

Thumby digs in.
Doesn't get any better than this, sports fans.
Two outs, ducks on the pond.

Steee-rike one!

Oh-and-two on Thumby.
Doesn't look good for the Webbies.

Here's the wind-up, and...here's the pitch.
Thumby swings—

Webbies win!

For the first time this century!

INNING	1	2	3	4	5	6	7	8	9	RUNS
QUACKERS	0	0	1	0	0	0	0	2	0	3
WEBBIES	0	0	0	0	0	0	0	0	4	4

Listen to the cheers

for Thumby Duckling!

Four things ducks know about baseball:

1) Some games you win
2) Some you lose
3) And some you can't remember
4) But baseball is always lots of fun.